Haitian heroes: Catherine Flon (top);
Sanité Bélair (bottom); Jean-Jacques Dessalines
(far right, top); Toussaint Louverture (far right,
bottom).

Groundwood Books / House of Anansi Press
groundwoodbooks.com

We acknowledge for their financial support of our
publishing program the Canada Council for the Arts, the
Ontario Arts Council and the Government of Canada.

Canada Council   Conseil des Arts
for the Arts   du Canada

 ONTARIO ARTS COUNCIL
CONSEIL DES ARTS DE L'ONTARIO
an Ontario government agency
un organisme du gouvernement de l'Ontario

With the participation of the Government of Canada   Canadä
Avec la participation du gouvernement du Canada

Library and Archives Canada Cataloguing in Publication
Latour, Francie, author
Auntie Luce's talking paintings / Francie Latour ;
illustrated by Ken Daley.
Issued in print and electronic formats.
ISBN 978-1-77306-041-5 (hardcover). —
ISBN 978-1-77306-042-2 (PDF)
I. Daley, Ken, illustrator II. Title.
PZ7.1.L38Aun 2018   j813'.6   C2018-900442-8
C2018-900443-6

The art was rendered in acrylic on illustration board.
Design by Michael Solomon
Printed and bound in Malaysia

To my three loves, my little people
growing so fast —
Owen Sky, Riley Rose and Leo Satchel.
Haiti belongs to you, too. FL

To my niece Vada. KD

AUNTIE LUCE'S TALKING PAINTINGS

Francie Latour

Pictures by **Ken Daley**

GROUNDWOOD BOOKS
HOUSE OF ANANSI PRESS
TORONTO   BERKELEY

In my mother's bedroom, behind the family pictures and the jar that holds her wedding-day flowers, a painting sits on a shelf.

It's a painting of me, my eyes almost closed, like I'm dreaming. My braids hang like coal-colored ropes. My face fills the frame, so big and so close that if you look long enough, it starts to look like a whole land — brown hills melting into yellow valleys melting into red riverbeds, and even the rivers' silver light, running smooth over the rocks.

When I think back to the first time my auntie Luce painted me, I lose myself in the memory of people and places she brings to life with her brushes — fortresses in high cliffs and crayon-colored boats by the sea, gingerbread houses, and coconuts poked with straws for coconut water.

When I want to hear the stories of Haiti, the place where my mother was born, I talk to Auntie Luce's paintings.

The paintings always talk back.

My mother says I was too young to remember
Auntie Luce painting me.
"You were only seven. Ou kwè ou sonje jou sa a?"
But I do remember ...

It is December, the time of year when I leave the
snow and snowman-making behind. I step onto an
airplane, and when I step off again a wall of heat
wraps my body and instantly warms my blood.

Inside the airport, Auntie Luce waves me to her, and the metal bracelets along her arms start to sing. My first question is always the same.

"Can I sit for you, Auntie Luce? Will you paint me this time, please?"

"Ti Chouchou, ou fè kè m kontan," she says, cupping my cheeks but not answering my question.

She opens the trunk and makes room for my suitcase, pushing the palettes and clinking jars to one side. Then we drive through city streets, and familiar scenes fly by my open window.

There go the boys selling water ice by the pink cathedral. There go the market women balancing fruit baskets on their heads. There go the tap tap buses painted with soccer stars and signs that say, "Se Ginen Nou Ye." We are the children of Guinea, of West Africa.

Soon the city falls under our feet, and fog carpets the mountain road to the house. As we climb the hills, a question comes to me.

"When Mom left for the States, why didn't you come?"

"Your mother and I are different, Ti Chou," she says. "When I close my eyes for good, I want Haiti to be the last thing I see."

I help bring in the easels and sacks filled with paint tubes and rags. Auntie Luce doesn't waste any time quizzing me on last year's lessons.

"Ayiti, the land of mountains. That was the name of this place before the Europeans came." She snaps vanilla beans into a pot of oatmeal. "Before the Spanish and the French. *Before*, before. Your mother — she doesn't tell you these stories?"

At home, my parents play old konpa records with friends late into the night. They argue over how Haiti got broken and how it can be fixed. My brother and I listen from the top of the stairs.

"They tell stories about crooked presidents and bad armies," I say. "Is that true?"

Auntie Luce slides a placemat onto the table and sets down the bowl.

"The truth is a hard thing to untangle," she says, "like a big knot of yarn. To tell the truth about this place — this tiny, tiny place — you have to look at its strong, powerful neighbor. You have to look at America."

We put black mushrooms in a pot to soak
for dinner. Then we tie on our smocks and
take a familiar walk — down the stone path,
past the chickens and the garden of choublak
flowers, into Auntie Luce's studio.

Inside, Haiti's heroes greet me — Bélair and Flon, her head wrapped in white, her needle stitching a new flag for a free nation. I see Dessalines and Louverture, the general who found a way to win and forced Napoleon back across the ocean.

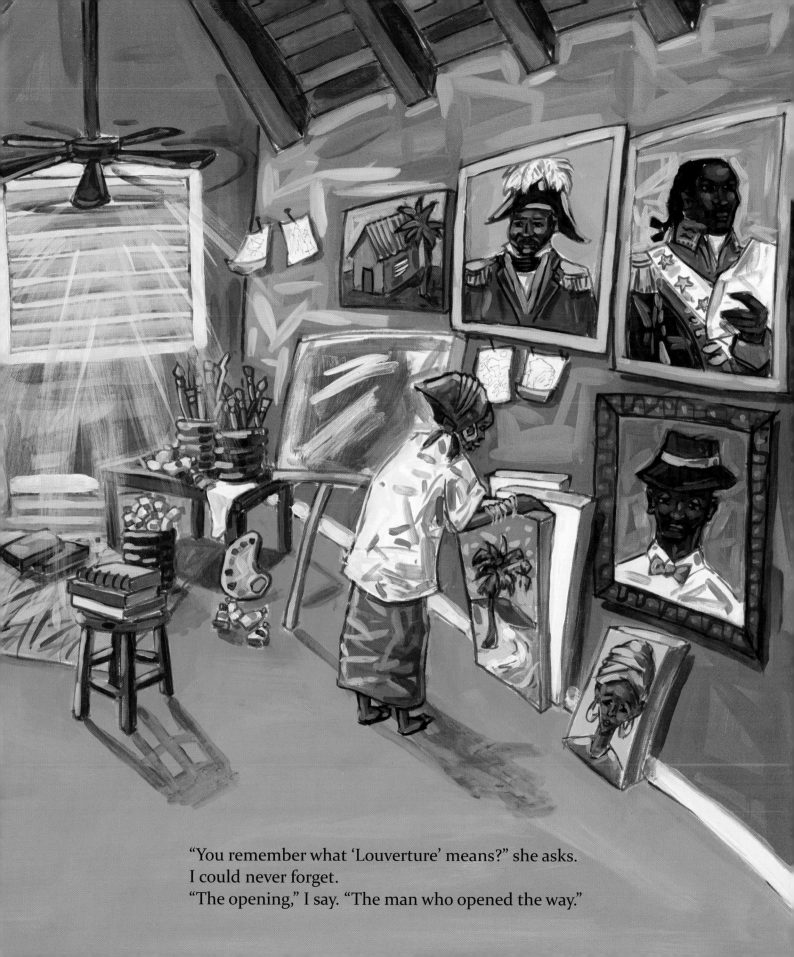

"You remember what 'Louverture' means?" she asks.
I could never forget.
"The opening," I say. "The man who opened the way."

My own heroes are here, too. My grandfather, the
tailor who made suits for the businessmen in town.

My great-grandmother, who wore her hair parted in two buns and went blind from old age. If these paintings could talk, I wonder, what would they tell me? With my slow, broken Kreyòl, would they know I am their daughter?

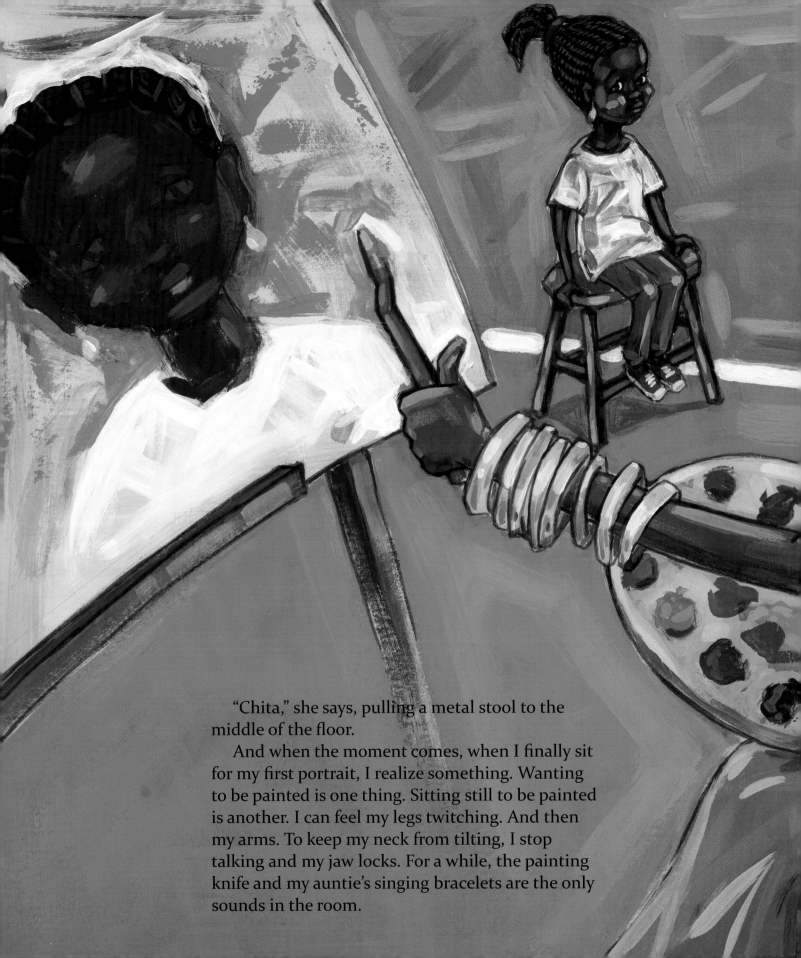

"Chita," she says, pulling a metal stool to the
middle of the floor.
And when the moment comes, when I finally sit
for my first portrait, I realize something. Wanting
to be painted is one thing. Sitting still to be painted
is another. I can feel my legs twitching. And then
my arms. To keep my neck from tilting, I stop
talking and my jaw locks. For a while, the painting
knife and my auntie's singing bracelets are the only
sounds in the room.

"Do you know why I paint, Ti Chou?" she asks after a long silence.

I've never thought about that.

"Because you're good at it?"

She laughs deep in her throat, then mixes more reds and browns.

"Because Haiti is so beautiful?" I ask.

"Not always," she says. "Sometimes, it's almost too hard to look at."

"I paint to remember what I've seen and heard and smelled and felt. The balconies wrapped around houses, which seem to go on forever, the fists pounding on neighborhood doors and sending people into hiding.

"To paint Haiti takes the darkest colors and the brightest ones, and all the colors in between."

In two days of sitting, Auntie Luce paints me from
many different angles. On one easel, I can see myself
turned completely to the side.

In my face, I see colors I've never seen in a mirror —
the caramel in my great-grandmother's skin and the deep
berry in my grandfather's. I see the colors of metal roofs
over houses with no upstairs or downstairs. I see the ash
of earthquake dust, from that time the ground shook and
opened up.

Auntie Luce says our faces are like maps.
"I can trace yours halfway around
the world, from the kingdoms of Benin
to the sugarcane fields that turned into
battlefields, where we fought to the death
for our freedom," she says. "All the way to
this room, in this light."

I gather the brushes in a rag and follow my aunt to the washroom. Over the sink, I let the colors bleed together in the water, ash to cocoa to rust, butterscotch to nut, and nut to clay.

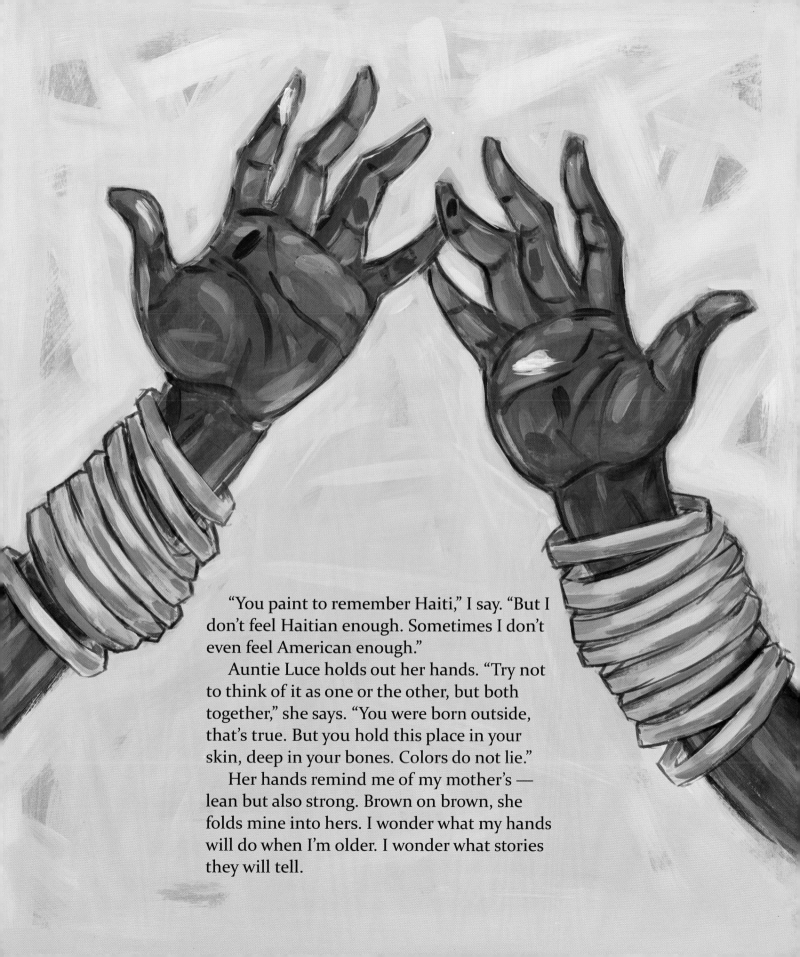

"You paint to remember Haiti," I say. "But I don't feel Haitian enough. Sometimes I don't even feel American enough."

Auntie Luce holds out her hands. "Try not to think of it as one or the other, but both together," she says. "You were born outside, that's true. But you hold this place in your skin, deep in your bones. Colors do not lie."

Her hands remind me of my mother's — lean but also strong. Brown on brown, she folds mine into hers. I wonder what my hands will do when I'm older. I wonder what stories they will tell.

"Can I take it home, Auntie Luce? Can I keep the portrait?"

"Ti Chou," she says, "it's yours. These colors, this people, this place belong to you. And you belong to them, always."

AUTHOR'S NOTE

We all have birth stories. In my family, we tell them often: my brother, the "miracle baby," born so early he wasn't expected to survive, much less thrive at six feet tall; my daughter, the daredevil, who could not wait to meet the world and shot out like a cannon, with people to see, places to go and things to do.

Nations have birth stories, too. And though few people know it, the two countries at the heart of Ti Chou's world — Haiti and the United States — were both born from the same fire: revolutions for freedom that changed the world.

Only one of these revolutions is taught in school — a band of colonies that overthrew British rule, a heroic general named Washington, and a new nation of free citizens we now call America. But just a few years later and a little farther south, a band of rebels on an island called Saint-Domingue also defeated a powerful European ruler. They, too, had a heroic general, named Louverture, and a declaration of independence from France under the emperor Napoleon.

When these rebels birthed a nation and called it Haiti, the whole world paid attention. Why? Because these new citizens — who beat the French, the Spanish and the British — were Black, descended from Africans who were forced across an ocean and into an inhuman system of slavery.

The Haitian Revolution (1791–1804) did more than overthrow a government. It overthrew an *idea*, one that Europeans invented and had to protect to keep slavery going: that they were "White," that Africans were "Black," and that Blacks were somehow inferior — less human, or not human at all. As long as this idea stayed in place, Europeans and Americans could use the forced labor of others to become wealthy world powers. They could write birth stories of freedom and democracy in our history books, despite keeping generations of Black people in chains.

For proving these ideas wrong, Haiti would be punished. From the moment this Black republic was born, it was totally alone in the world. No country would trade with it or even recognize it as a nation. To get that recognition, Haiti had to sign a deal that guaranteed a future of poverty. It was forced to pay hundreds of millions to the French for the property they lost in war — an amount that today is worth about $20 billion. That lost property included Haitians' very own bodies, which the French believed they had a right to own.

Growing up, the only stories I heard about Haiti in school were that it was violent and poor, one of the poorest countries on Earth. And this is why knowing our birth stories is so important to understanding the world, and each other.